CREATED AND WRITTEN BY
Charles Arthur Blount

ILLUSTRATIONS BY
Pedro J.du Buf

EDITED BY
Charlayne S. Blount

Library of Congress Cataloging-in-publication Data is on file with the publisher.

ISBN: 978-1-66783-344-6

"Come now all as I tell you a story,
About a man from nowhere
that was searching for glory.

"A cautionary tale about life and the danger,
Of not following your heart
and listening to strangers."

In a place round the bend, past the lake and further down,
Lived the people of Perfect, a quaint and cozy Southern town.
The people of Perfect were a strong and noble group.
Perfect boasted no crime, honest people and reverent youth.

On a stormy day around the middle of May,
the people of Perfect were in for dismay;
The wind had gathered something and blew him their way.

THE CITY
OF
PERFECT

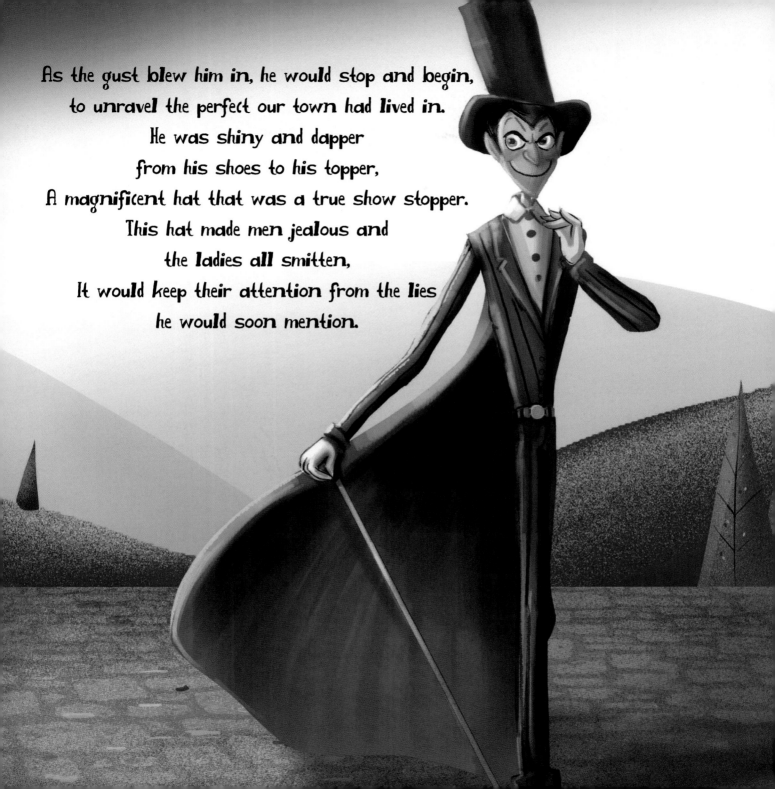

As the gust blew him in, he would stop and begin,
to unravel the perfect our town had lived in.
He was shiny and dapper
from his shoes to his topper,
A magnificent hat that was a true show stopper.
This hat made men jealous and
the ladies all smitten,
It would keep their attention from the lies
he would soon mention.

He stood in the corner of this town's tiny square.
"I have come here to warn you! You must listen and prepare!"
"I have come here to inform you! I have come to announce!"
"There will be many changes to this town you'll soon denounce!"

The people grew restless. What could he mean?
Things are so perfect in Perfect or at least that's what it seems!

What is this revolution that
he is announcing?
Will people be punching
and fighting and pouncing?

"Tell us new friend for what you have seen?"
"What is your vision?"
"What does this all mean?"

The man stood tall and proud and proclaimed,
"My friends you must trust me!"
"It's coming!"

"The Change!"

The people of Perfect looked hard at each other,
"Is it you?" "Is it him?"

"Is it Sally's strange brother?"

As the fingers were wagging and pointing directions
the people of Perfect began their insurrection!
Chaos ensued as all came unglued, the people of Perfect
had begun a full blown FEUD!

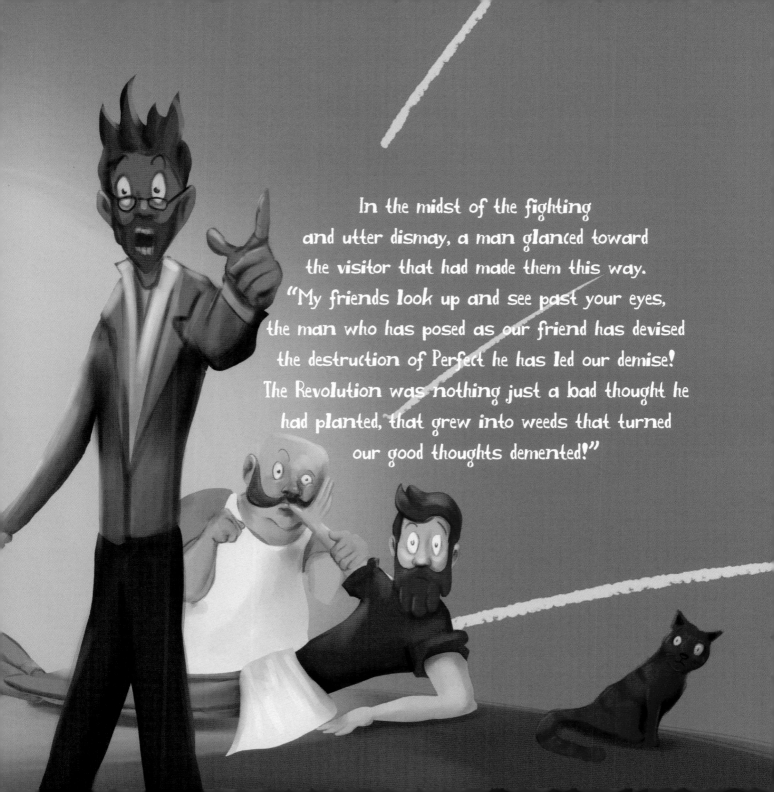

In the midst of the fighting
and utter dismay, a man glanced toward
the visitor that had made them this way.
"My friends look up and see past your eyes,
the man who has posed as our friend has devised
the destruction of Perfect he has led our demise!
The Revolution was nothing just a bad thought he
had planted, that grew into weeds that turned
our good thoughts demented!"

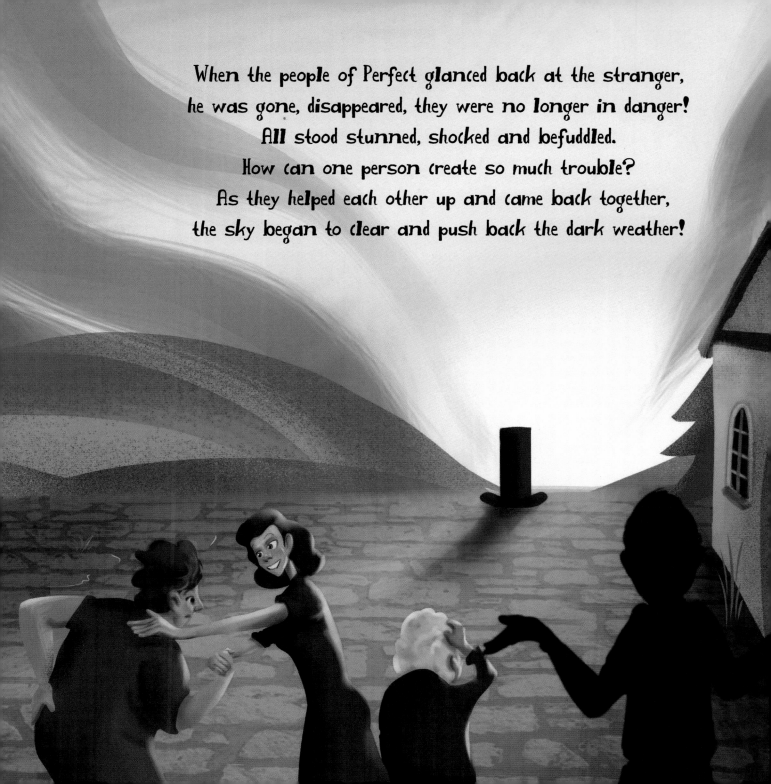

When the people of Perfect glanced back at the stranger,
he was gone, disappeared, they were no longer in danger!
All stood stunned, shocked and befuddled.
How can one person create so much trouble?
As they helped each other up and came back together,
the sky began to clear and push back the dark weather!

They looked and they searched for him behind this and around that!
But after all of their efforts all they found was his
big fabulous hat!

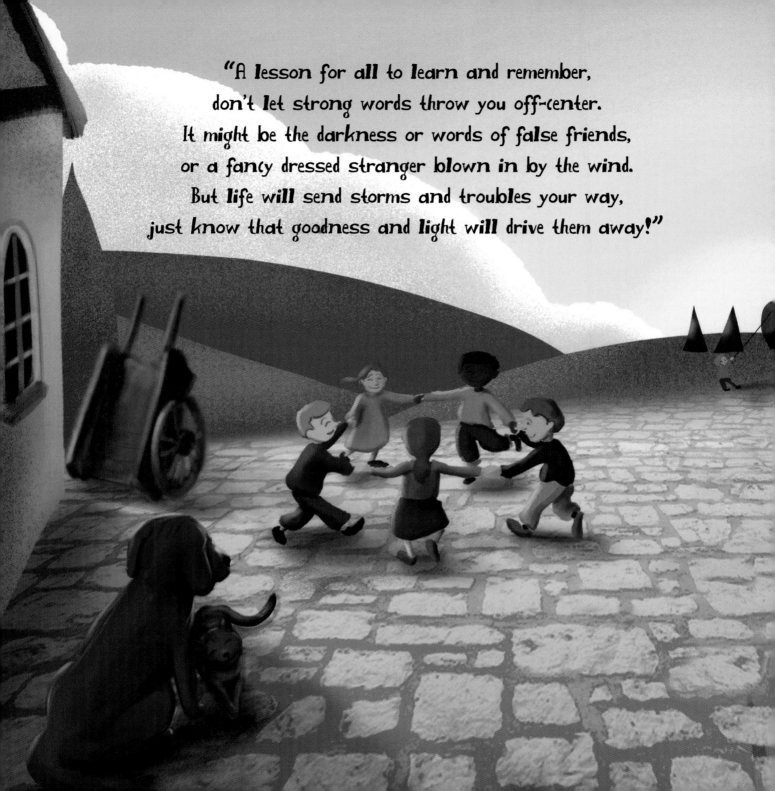

"A lesson for all to learn and remember,
don't let strong words throw you off-center.
It might be the darkness or words of false friends,
or a fancy dressed stranger blown in by the wind.
But life will send storms and troubles your way,
just know that goodness and light will drive them away!"

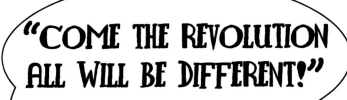

Written for Dad
on his 75th birthday,
to show how much I love him
because I would often hear him say;
"Come The Revolution All Will Be Different!"
We were never quite sure just exactly
what he meant...